Encyclopedia Fantastic Fish

This book will tell you about some fantastic fish.

For each fish, you will find:

a photo

a fantastic fact

The porcupine fish blows up like a balloon to look big and scary.

a map to show where it lives

a scale to show size

2-6 inches

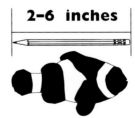

Rigby

Anglerfish

The anglerfish uses **bait** to fish for its dinner. The anglerfish has a fin that looks like a worm. When other fish see the fin, they come close. Then the anglerfish catches them!

1-2 feet

fin used for bait

Blind Catfish

Blind catfish don't need eyes, because they live in dark caves. Blind catfish use their whiskers to find food and to feel where they are going.

Southern United States

10 inches

Clownfish

Clownfish live between the **tentacles** of **sea anemones**. The tentacles have poison, which protects the clownfish from enemies.

2-6 inches

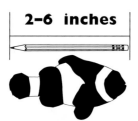

4

Dwarf Goby

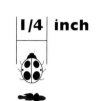

1/4 inch

The dwarf goby is the size of a ladybug.
It is the smallest fish in the world.

Philippines

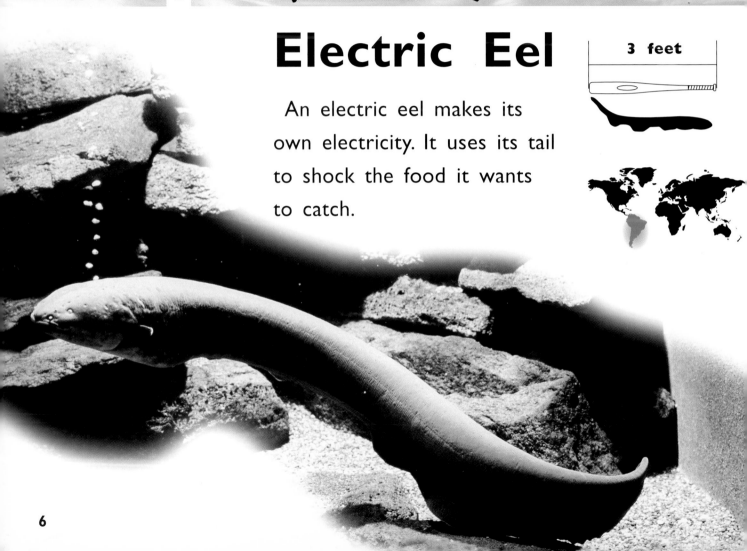

Electric Eel

3 feet

An electric eel makes its own electricity. It uses its tail to shock the food it wants to catch.

Frogfish

Frogfish live among the rocks on the bottom of the ocean. Instead of swimming, they use their fins to hop along.

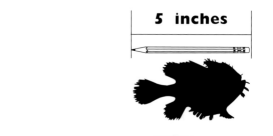

5 inches

Grunt

A grunt grinds its teeth, which makes a sound like a pig. Two grunts may swim with their red mouths together. That is why they are also called kissing fish.

1 foot

1 2 3 4 5 6 7 8 9 10 11 12

Hammerhead Shark

The hammerhead shark has an odd-shaped head. The hammer shape helps it make sharp turns in the water.

13 feet

Koi

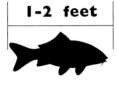

1-2 feet

Koi can live to be 100 years old. They were first grown in Japan for their beauty. Now they are kept in garden ponds everywhere.

Lanternfish

The lanternfish has lights on its head and body. It lives in the darkest parts of the ocean. The lanternfish uses the lights to **lure** little fish closer to eat.

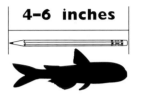

4-6 inches

lights

Cook Islands, Pacific Ocean

Lionfish

The lionfish has fins that contain poison. The fins can quickly kill a much bigger fish.

16 inches

fins

12

Manta Ray

Manta rays have fins that look like wings. Although they look big and mean, manta rays are gentle and graceful.

22 feet

Mudskipper

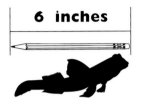

6 inches

Mudskippers can walk on land. They use their fins like crutches to skip across the muddy shore. Mudskippers eat insects living in the mud.

14

Ocean Sunfish

Ocean sunfish float at the top of the ocean to sun themselves. Ocean sunfish can lay more eggs than any other fish. One fish can lay 30 million eggs at a time. Each egg is smaller than the head of a pin.

11 feet

Piranha

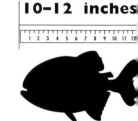

Piranhas have teeth like **razors**. They eat animals that get in the river. Piranhas also eat fruit and seeds.

Porcupine Fish

The porcupine fish blows up like a balloon to look big and scary. It is covered with poisonous spines. The spines protect the porcupine fish from bigger fish.

10–12 inches

Russian Sturgeon

The Russian sturgeon's eggs are very valuable. People like to eat the eggs, which are called caviar. One fish can produce 50 pounds of eggs.

4 feet

Black and Caspian Seas

18

Sailfish

A sailfish can swim as fast as a cheetah can run. It is the fastest fish in the ocean.

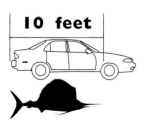

10 feet

Salmon

Salmon are strong enough to swim upstream against rushing water and jump up waterfalls. They live in the ocean, but they swim up rivers to lay their eggs in the same place where they were born.

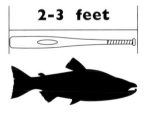

2-3 feet

Trumpetfish

The tube-shaped trumpetfish stands on its head, waiting to suck up **prey** that comes too close. The trumpetfish looks just like the coral in which it hides.

trumpetfish

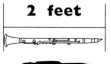

2 feet

21

Whale Shark

The world's biggest fish has the smallest teeth. The whale shark has 300 rows of tiny teeth, which are useless for catching food. Instead, the whale shark uses gills like a net to scoop up **plankton**.

40 feet

Glossary

bait food that is used to catch fish

lure to invite

plankton tiny plants and animals that float in water

prey an animal hunted for food

razor a very sharp, cutting tool

sea anemone a brightly colored animal that looks like a flower with tentacles around its mouth

tentacles long, flexible arms